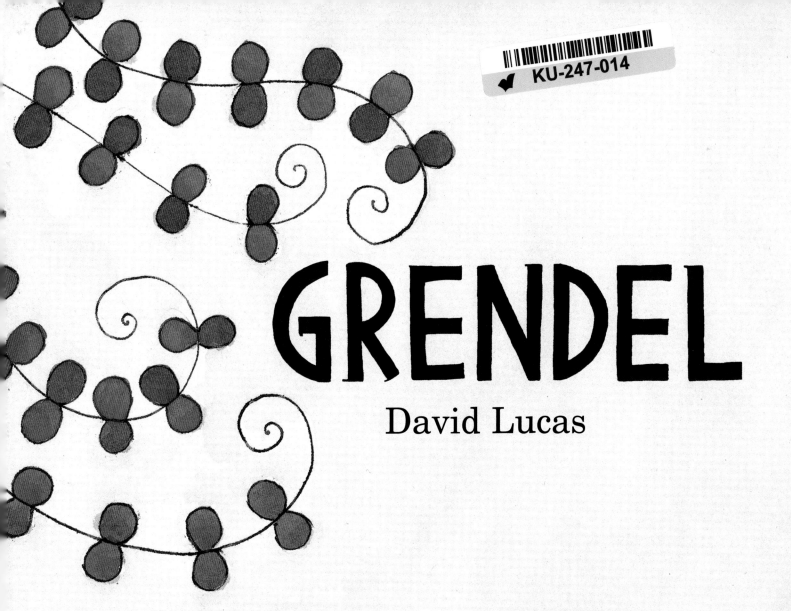

GRENDEL

David Lucas

First published 2013 by Walker Books Ltd, 87 Vauxhall Walk, London SE11 5HJ
1 2 3 4 5 6 7 8 9 10 © 2013 David Lucas. The right of David Lucas to be identified as author/illustrator of this work has been asserted by him in accordance with the Copyright, Designs and Patents Act 1988. This book has been typeset in New Century Schoolbook. Printed in China. All rights reserved. No part of this book may be reproduced, transmitted or stored in an information retrieval system in any form or by any means, graphic, electronic or mechanical, including photocopying, taping and recording, without prior written permission from the publisher. British Library Cataloguing in Publication Data: a catalogue record for this book is available from the British Library. ISBN 978-1-4063-3909-3 www.walker.co.uk

WALKER BOOKS
AND SUBSIDIARIES
LONDON · BOSTON · SYDNEY · AUCKLAND

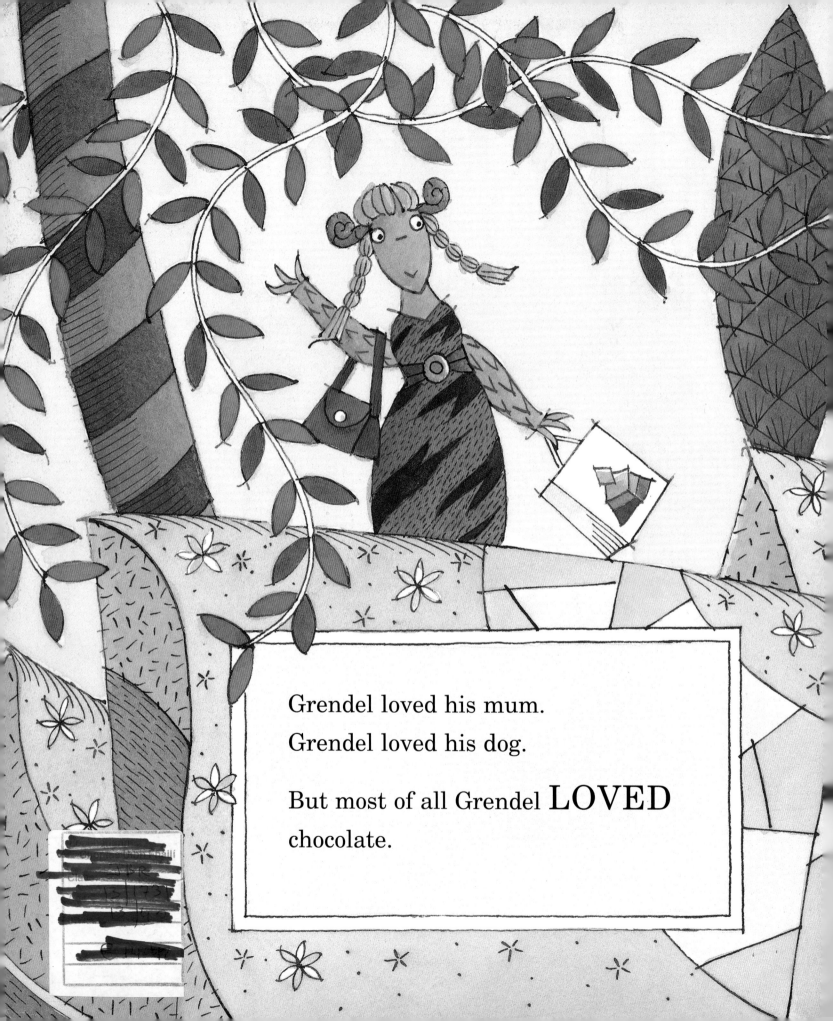

Grendel loved his mum.
Grendel loved his dog.

But most of all Grendel LOVED chocolate.

To Astrid and Helena

"I bought you a chocolate egg,"
said Grendel's mum.

"CHOCOLATE!"
said Grendel.
"Give it to me!
Give it to me!"

"I was only going to
give it to you if
you were good,"
said Mum.

"I'll be good.
        I'll be good..."

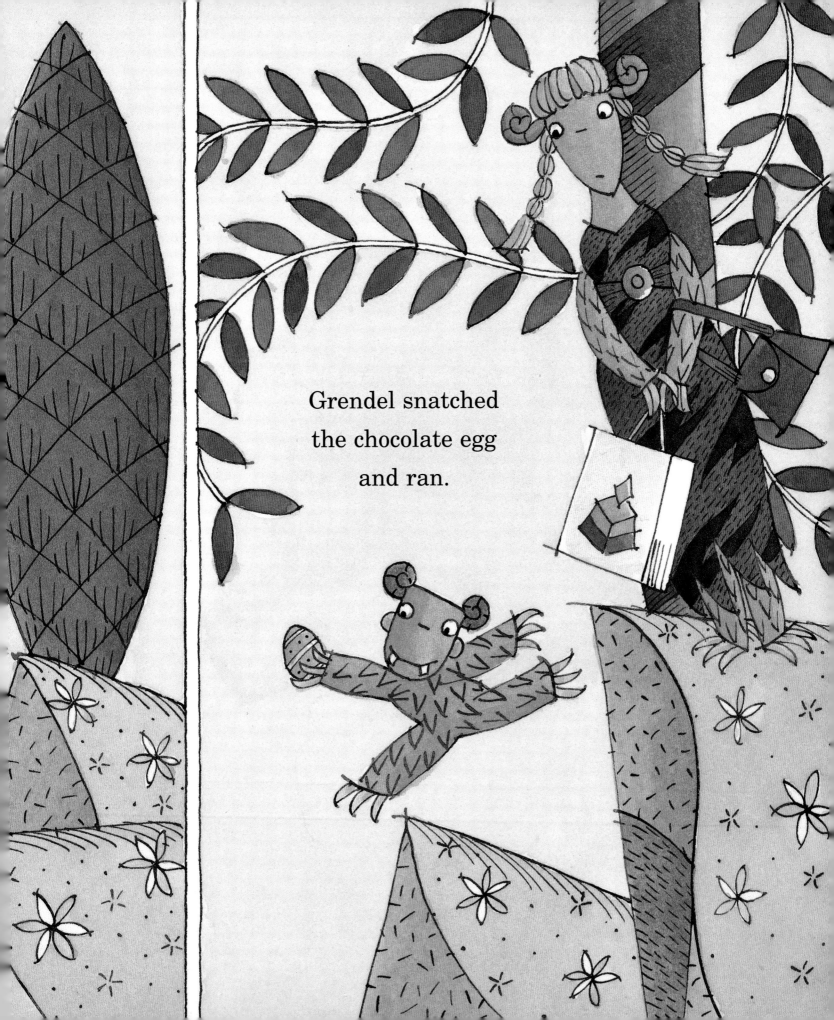

Grendel snatched
the chocolate egg
and ran.

He sat in his secret hiding place.

Mmm ... *delicious*.

He was just about to wish the WHOLE WORLD
was chocolate when he stopped...
No. He had to be SENSIBLE.

"I know!" he said.
"I wish ... everything
I *touch* turns
to chocolate!"

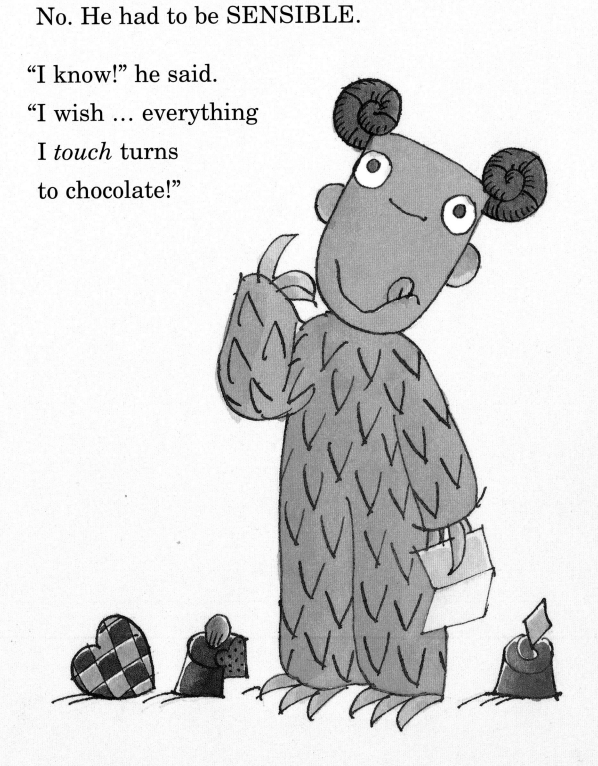

The note was chocolate.
YUM!
He was sitting on a chocolate log.
SNAP!
MMM.

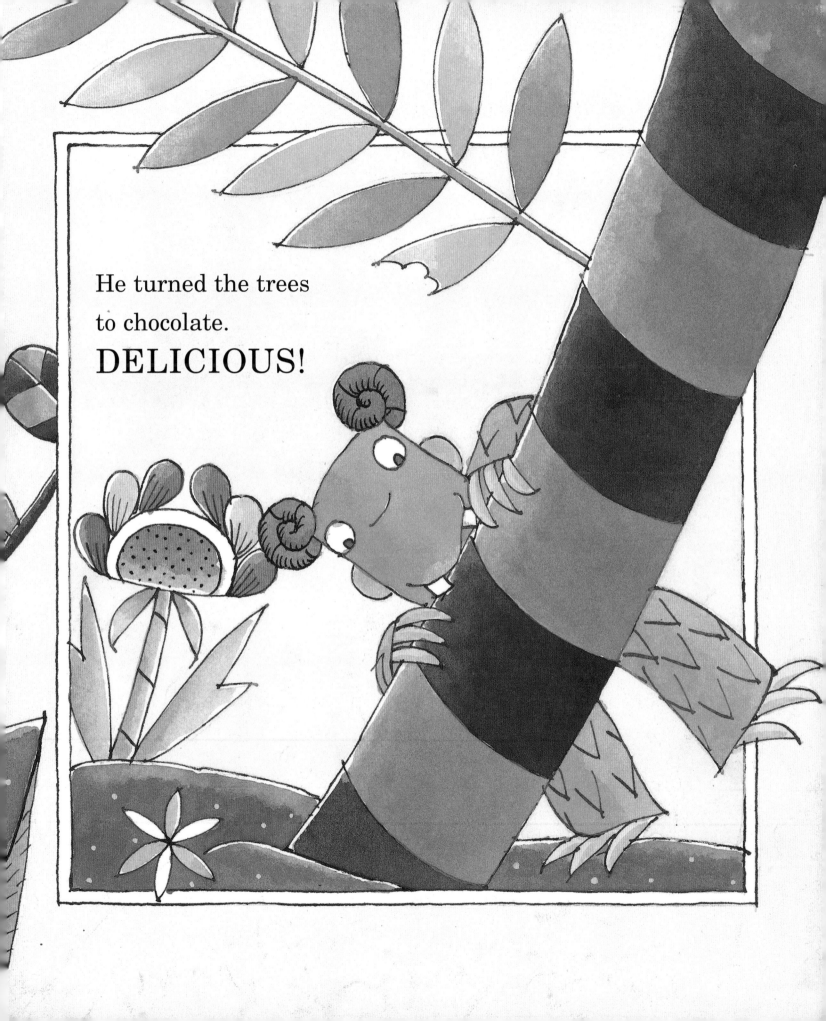

He turned the trees
to chocolate.
DELICIOUS!

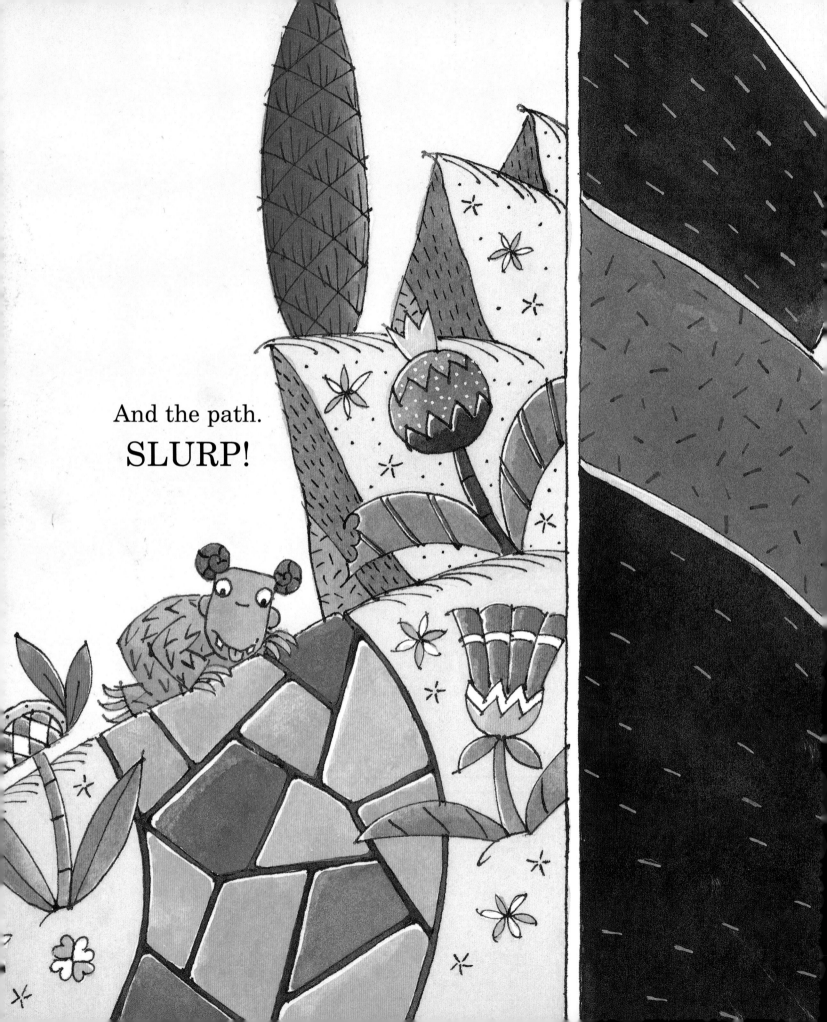

And the path.
SLURP!

And the rocks.
CRUNCH!

It was so much fun …

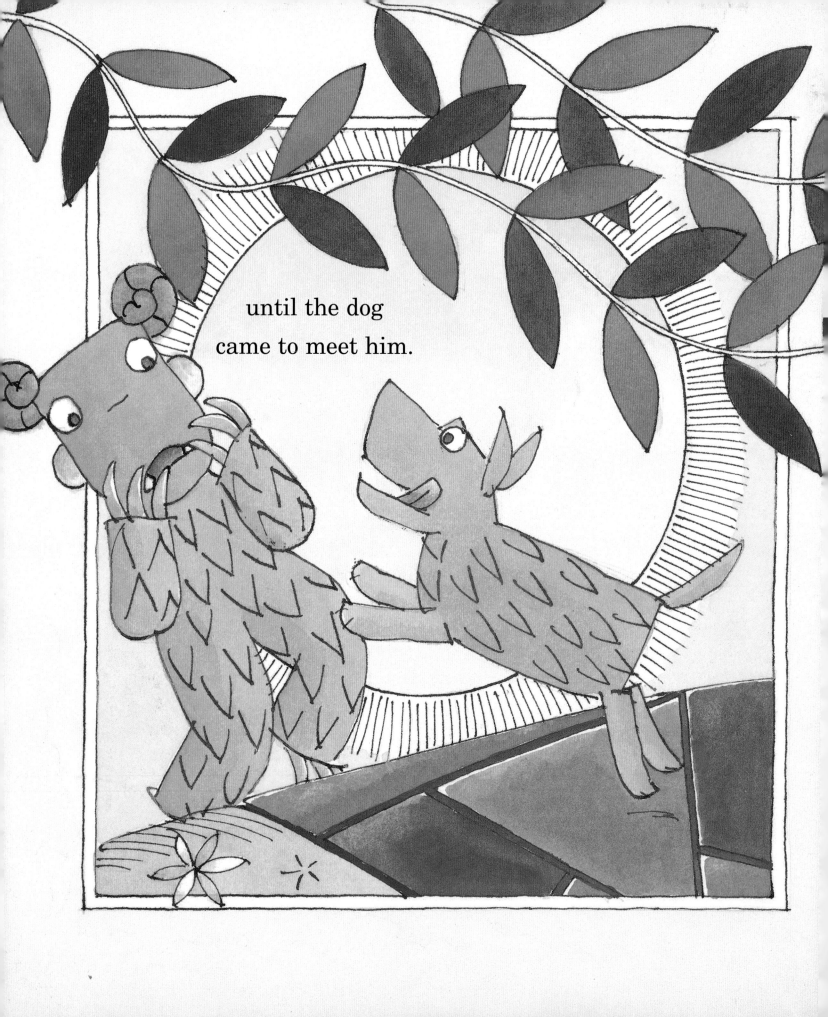

until the dog
came to meet him.

"NO!" said Grendel.

"Grendel!
What have you done?"
said Mum.

"NOOOO!!" said Grendel.
"Mum! Mum! Speak to me, Mum!"
But she didn't say a word.

"I *hate* chocolate!"
he roared.
"I hate it!
I hate it!
I HATE it!"

The sun was hot.
Mum ... was ...
starting ... to ...
melt!

"What have I done?" said Grendel.
He was just about to say that
he wished he wasn't so stupid
– when he stopped...

"I've got *one more* wish!
Think, Grendel, think. *Carefully*."

He had an idea. He closed his eyes
and crossed his claws.
"I wish ...

"it was ... YESTERDAY!"

His pillow wasn't chocolate.
Or his blanket.

He heard singing.

What a wonderful, familiar sound!

"Mum!" he cried.
"You're not chocolate!"
"Me? Chocolate?"
she laughed.
"No, dear."

He hugged her for a
long, long time. And then
he hugged the dog.

"What's happened to you?"
she said.
"You're so different!"
Then she smiled.
"You are a good little
monster really."

"Look, I bought you a
chocolate egg!"
"You have it," said Grendel.
"*Grendel?* Are you sure?"
"Yes, Mum. But if
there's a little
note inside…"

There WAS a little note inside.
"YOU HAVE THREE WISHES."

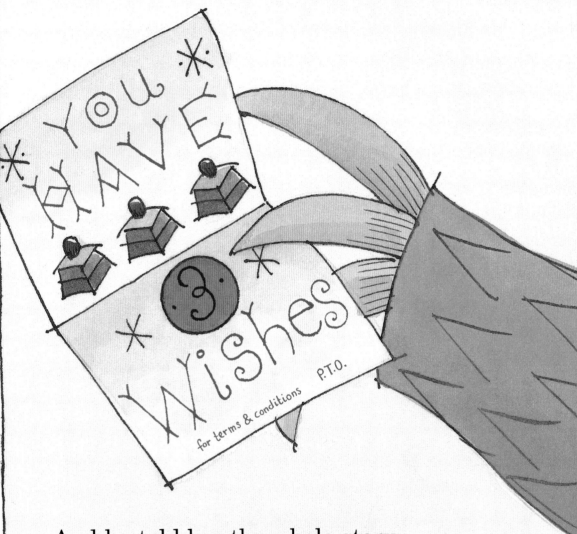

And he told her the whole story.
And of course the moral of this story
is to be careful what you wish for.

And they were …